Three kids, one friendship, and a bunch of crazy adventures!

Coming soon:
#2 Josh Taylor, Mr. Average

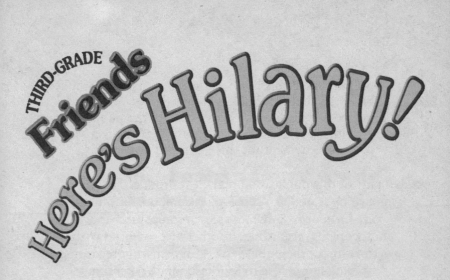

THIRD-GRADE Friends

Here's Hilary!

by Suzanne
Williams

Illustrated by
George Ulrichsen

A
LITTLE APPLE
PAPERBACK

SCHOLASTIC INC.

New York   Toronto   London   Auckland   Sydney
Mexico City   New Delhi   Hong Kong   Buenos Aires

No part of this publication may be reproduced in whole or
in part, or stored in a retrieval system, or transmitted in
any form or by any means, electronic, mechanical,
photocopying, recording, or otherwise, without written
permission of the publisher. For information regarding
permission, write to Scholastic Inc., Attention:
Permissions Department,
557 Broadway, New York, NY 10012.

ISBN 0-439-32988-4

Text copyright © 2002 by Suzanne Williams.
Illustrations copyright © 2002 by Scholastic Inc.
All rights reserved. Published by Scholastic Inc.
SCHOLASTIC, LITTLE APPLE PAPERBACKS, and
associated logos are trademarks and/or registered
trademarks of Scholastic Inc.

12 11 10 9 8 7 6 5 4   4 5 6 7 8/0
                                       40

Printed in the U.S.A.
First Scholastic printing, September 2002

To Vivian Sathre, Sylvie Hossack, Donna Bergman and Katherine Kirkpatrick, my wonderful writing group. Thanks for all your help!

And to Sallie Schuler, Cheri Pigott and Jan Murphy, the best library assistants ever.

Contents

1
Late Again

"Hilary?" Mom's voice on the other side of my bedroom door woke me. She rattled the doorknob. "Are you up?"

"Don't come in," I yelled, rolling over. "I'm getting dressed." I hopped out of bed so I wouldn't be telling a lie.

I checked my alarm clock. Argh! I'd overslept again. Maybe the alarm was broken.

But probably I'd just shut it off and gone back to sleep. I *hate* getting up early. Especially on Monday mornings.

I kicked through the pile of clothes on my floor, trying to find something to wear to school. My yellow dress looked clean, but I wanted to play wall-ball at recess. Playing wall-ball in a dress is like having to smile when you know you've got something stuck in your braces. You worry too much about what'll show.

Finally, I found a pair of pants that weren't *too* dirty. But my cleanest T-shirt had a big spaghetti stain on it. I opened my door and yelled down the hall. "Hey, Mom! I don't have any clean shirts!"

"I just did the laundry a couple of days ago," Mom called back. "There wasn't anything in your basket."

Grrr. Couldn't she tell which clothes on the floor were dirty? I sighed and put on the T-shirt with the spaghetti stain.

Mom was feeding something disgusting looking to my baby sister, Melanie, when I came into the kitchen. I'm glad *I'm* not a baby anymore. I got myself a bowl of Corn Crunchies and sat down to eat.

"No, no, Melanie," Mom was saying. "Don't spit out your food, sweetie. Swallow it."

If *I* had to eat what Melanie eats, I'd spit it out, too. She probably wishes she were nine like me so she could eat Corn Crunchies instead. A blob of yellowy-brown stuff flew out of Melanie's mouth and landed on Mom's blouse.

"Yuck," Mom said, wiping it off. "So much for this blouse."

Suddenly, I wasn't hungry anymore. I dumped my half-finished bowl of cereal in the sink and ran downstairs to look for my homework. I was sure I'd left it on the coffee table last night.

"Mom!" I shouted as I came up the stairs. "Have you seen my homework?"

"No, dear," Mom called from down the hall.

I'd lost my watch a week ago, so I wasn't sure what time it was, but I knew if I didn't leave soon I'd be late. And my third grade teacher, Ms. Foster, didn't like it when I was late. In fact, last Friday she'd said that if I was late one more time she'd have to "take steps."

I decided to forget about finding my homework. Ms. Foster wasn't going to like that, either, but what else could I do? I grabbed my backpack and headed out the door.

Halfway down the block I realized I'd left my lunch on the kitchen counter. I can't *live* without lunch, so I ran back and snatched it off the counter. "Bye!" I yelled, slamming out the door again.

As I hurried to school, I thought about my friend Josh. He's always teasing me about being tardy and forgetting stuff. He says if my head wasn't stuck between my shoulders, I wouldn't *have* one, because I'd walk off and leave it somewhere. Or just forget where I put it. I'd never admit it to him, but sometimes I think he's right.

Puffing hard, I jogged the rest of the way to school. Near the edge of the playground sits this portable classroom that looks like a little square house and is separate from the rest of the school. Just as I passed it, the bell rang.

Double argh! All I could do was go straight to the office and pick up a tardy slip — again. I shuddered. I had a feeling I was about to find out the exact meaning of Ms. Foster's "take steps."

2
Time Tests

Luckily for me, Ms. Foster was at the chalkboard when I walked into class, so I didn't have to find out about those "steps" right away. I dropped my tardy slip on her desk and sat down.

A voice at my elbow made me jump. Josh had crept up from his seat at the back of the room. "I used to think turtles were slow," he whispered, crouching next to my desk. "But if you raced one to school, I bet I know who'd win."

"Very funny," I said. "Remind me to get a dog if I ever need a *real* friend."

Josh grinned. We always tease and insult each other like that. It's kind of a game we play.

When Josh grins, his stick-out ears stick out even more. They look like two big mushrooms growing out of the sides of his head. He can make them wiggle just by concentrating, which is *so* cool.

"I'm going to beat you at wall-ball at recess today," Josh said.

I snorted. "That's what *you* think!"

Josh wiggled his ears at me. Then he sneaked back to his desk before Ms. Foster could notice he was out of his seat. Josh is always saying he's going to beat me at wall-ball, but he hardly ever does.

Gordon Cunningham started passing out the math time tests we take every Monday and Thursday. Everyone calls him a teacher's pet because Ms. Foster is always asking him to help. She's probably the only friend he has at school, he's such a bossy know-it-all. And most of the time he talks like a grown-up, using lots of big words *nobody* understands.

"The fact that you're still on Level A defies comprehension," Gordon said as he passed me my test. "I'm on Level G."

See what I mean? *"Defies comprehension?"*

Then Gordon made this tsking sound that reminds me of chickens pecking at seeds. I scowled at him. I can't help it if I'm just no good at time tests.

Ms. Foster faced the class. She was wearing jeans, like she usually does, with a bright blue T-shirt today. The outline of an open

book was stenciled on her shirt, and underneath were the words "Readers are leaders" in big red letters. Ms. Foster smoothed back her dark, frizzy hair, but it just popped up all wild again when she stopped. "Pencils ready, everyone?"

I searched inside my desk. There had to be a pencil in there somewhere.

"Ready. Set. Go!" Ms. Foster said.

Finally, I found a pencil, but the lead was broken. I pawed through my desk to find my sharpener, and my test fell onto the floor. I snatched it up, sharpened my pencil, and set to work. But I'd barely finished the second row of problems when Ms. Foster called time.

Gordon collected the tests. "Tsk, tsk," he said when I handed him my paper.

I gritted my teeth. He's *so* annoying. I bet when he was younger even his *imaginary* friends wouldn't play with him.

At morning recess I tried to slip out the door to the playground before Ms. Foster noticed I was leaving. But no such luck. "Hilary," she said, "we need to talk."

I tried to look surprised. "What about?"

Ms. Foster sighed and held up my tardy slip. "You've been late to school *five times* in the last two weeks."

"Yes, I know." I gave her a little smile. "The school's always ringing that bell before I can get here."

Ms. Foster didn't laugh. She eyed the spaghetti stain on my T-shirt. "It's not just the tardiness, Hilary. You're behind on the time tests, and several assignments are missing."

"Which ones?" I asked. "They might be in my backpack. Or maybe my desk."

Ms. Foster just gave me a look. "After lunch, I'm sending you to talk with the principal. Dr. Wentworth is the most organized person I know. She'll be able to help you for sure."

I groaned. How could Dr. Wentworth help me? Would she find my missing assignments? Walk me to school? Take my time tests for me?

The morning recess was almost over, and Josh had wanted me to play wall-ball. What was I supposed to tell him? If he knew what was happening, he'd *really* give me a bad time. I could just hear him now. "Hilary," he'd say, "if you left your brain to science, no one would take it." Argh!

3
Dr. Wentworth

"Come right this way, please." Mrs. Crawford, the school secretary, held the door to the principal's office open for me.

My knees shook a little as I stepped inside. I'd never been in the principal's office before. I'd never even *talked* to Dr. Wentworth.

She looked up from her desk. The color of her hair matched the silver of the earrings and necklace she wore. "Please sit down, Hilary," she said.

"You know my name?" I was so impressed I forgot all about being nervous.

Dr. Wentworth smiled. She tapped a folder on her desk. "Your name is in here, on a note from your teacher. She says you need help getting organized. Is that right?"

I squirmed in my chair, not really wanting to talk about it. I don't like other people helping me. I never have. Mom says that once, when I was three, I threw a tantrum when she tried to tie my shoelaces. "I do it myself! I do it myself!" I screamed at her, even though I didn't know how to tie them.

"Well?" Dr. Wentworth was waiting for me to say something.

"I — I *am* late to school sometimes," I said finally. "And — and sometimes I can't find things right away."

"I see," Dr. Wentworth said. She tapped her fingertips together. "Maybe I can help by showing you how I keep track of everything *I* have to do."

"Okay," I said, feeling somewhat better. Maybe there was a trick to this organization thing. If I could learn it, everyone would leave me alone. It's not like I *like* being tardy and having to hunt for my homework.

Dr. Wentworth moved some papers on her desk. "Now, let me just show you . . ." She paused, frowning. "That's funny. I was certain that list was right here." She pressed the button on her intercom.

"Mrs. Crawford," she said. "Would you come in here, please?"

Mrs. Crawford poked her head in the door. "Yes, Dr. Wentworth?"

"Where is that to-do list you printed out

for me this morning?" Dr. Wentworth asked. "I can't seem to find it."

I put my hand over my mouth, covering a grin. Dr. Wentworth wasn't as organized as Ms. Foster thought. I wished I could tell Josh.

Mrs. Crawford glanced around the room. "Is that the list there? On top of your filing cabinet?" she asked.

"Ah, yes," said Dr. Wentworth, reaching up for it. "Thanks."

Dr. Wentworth showed me her list.

```
To Do List
Monday, September 23

* Visit Mr. Wasserman's
  kindergarten class
* 10:30 meeting with Dr. White
* Write principal's column for fall
  newsletter
* 1:00 4th grade assembly
* Review new math text books
* After-school Monday meeting
  with office staff
```

"Everything I need to do today is on this list," she said, pointing. "The key to organization is planning your work and working your plan." "But I thought *Mrs. Crawford* made the list," I said as politely as I could.

"She *typed* it," said Dr. Wentworth. "But I told her what needed to be on it."

"But Mrs. Crawford helped," I insisted. "And she knew where to find the list. She even brought you my file folder." Then before I could stop myself I said, "Too bad *I* don't have a secretary."

Even as I said it I knew it was the wrong thing to say. I hoped Dr. Wentworth wouldn't be mad at me. Sometimes I can't help pointing out the truth of things, even when it lands me in hot water.

A funny look came over her face. "You know what?" Dr. Wentworth said, "that's not a bad idea." She pressed the button on her intercom. "Mrs. Crawford, please ask Ms. Foster to send down her most organized student."

I wanted to hit myself for opening my big, fat mouth. And wouldn't you know, Ms. Foster sent *Gordon*.

4
The Deal

When Gordon stepped inside Dr. Wentworth's office, his eyes were as big as chicken eggs. He was probably scared he was in trouble or something. Shoot! I bet he's never been in trouble in his whole life.

Just looking at Gordon's chicken-egg eyes reminded me of his "tsk, tsk" chicken-pecking noises. And that's when I started to think of him as *Chicken Boy.*

Dr. Wentworth smiled at Chicken Boy. "Have a seat."

Holding himself stiff as a frozen Popsicle, Gordon edged into the chair next to mine.

As Dr. Wentworth explained about my "organization problem," Chicken Boy Gordon began to thaw out. I picked at my shoelaces, hoping Dr. Wentworth wouldn't say I'd *asked* for his help. Didn't she know I'd been kidding?

"So here's the deal, Gordon," Dr. Wentworth said at last. "If you'll be Hilary's secretary and help her make it through the rest of the week with no tardies and no missing assignments, I'll treat you both to lunch at the Pizza Pit."

Gordon looked over at me and grinned. "It's an acceptable arrangement," he said.

Dr. Wentworth was so unfair! No kid in

their right mind — even a kid like Gordon — could resist pizza.

I crossed my arms and scowled. I love pizza, and the Pizza Pit's double-cheese pizza is the absolute best, but I sure didn't want anyone's help. Especially Gordon's. Anyway, I was certain he didn't know the first thing about being a *real* secretary. He only liked the idea of bossing me around.

Dr. Wentworth looked at me. "All right with you, Hilary?"

Against my will, I nodded. What else *could* I do? Dr. Wentworth thought it was what I wanted. I didn't want to admit it was all a mistake. That I hadn't really meant it. "There's just one thing," I said. "No one needs to know about this, do they? Our deal can be a secret, right?"

Dr. Wentworth smiled. "The only people who need to know are you and Gordon and Ms. Foster and myself. You don't have to tell anyone else unless you want to."

"And Gordon can't tell anyone, either," I said.

"That seems fair," said Dr. Wentworth. "Can you agree to that, Gordon?"

Gordon nodded.

"Good." Dr. Wentworth got up from her

desk. "Come back to my office at the end of the week, and we'll see how you did."

As Gordon and I left, Dr. Wentworth called after us. "Good luck!"

I cringed.

"Listen, Gordon," I said as we walked back to class. "You heard what Dr. Wentworth said. This is a *secret* deal." I glared at him. "I won't say a word about this, and if *you* tell anyone, I'll break every bone in your body."

For a second, Chicken Boy really did look scared. Then he said, "Even if I wanted to, who would I tell?"

He had a point. His only friend, Ms. Foster, already knew.

When we got back to the classroom everyone was at Music. Gordon checked his watch. "We've got several minutes before the

25

rest of the class returns, so we might as well commence."

Before I could protest, he marched over to my desk and bent to inspect the inside. "Tsk, tsk. No wonder you can never find anything in here."

I frowned. Chicken Boy was pecking at seeds again. "Why don't *you* clean it," I asked, "since you're my secretary?"

"A satisfactory idea," he said. "Only I hope I don't dispose of something you want to keep."

Argh! I hadn't thought about *that*. "Never mind," I growled. "I'll do it."

While Chicken Boy watched, I pawed through my desk till I found yesterday's leftover sandwich and my empty glue bottle. I'd just crossed the room to throw them away when the class marched back in.

Josh came up to me at the garbage can. "Hey, I waited for you at recess," he said. "Where were you? Hiding out in the rest room so I wouldn't beat you?"

"Ha!" I avoided his question. "I could beat you with my eyes closed," I said instead. "In fact, you're so weak you couldn't lick an envelope."

Josh grinned. "Nice comeback."

Luckily he didn't have time to ask me again where I'd been because just then Ms. Foster signaled for everyone to get out their math books.

"Meet me at the wall-ball court at the next recess, okay?" Josh said. He raised an eyebrow. "And try not to get lost on the way."

"I'll draw myself a map," I said. Brushing sandwich crumbs off my hands, I headed back to my desk.

When it was time for afternoon recess I raced to the coatracks to grab my jacket. I was dying for a game.

Gordon stopped me at the racks. "You can't go yet," he said as all the other kids got their jackets and left.

I stared at him. "Why not?"

"You haven't finished cleaning your desk," he said.

I blinked. "What are you talking about? I'm done."

"Done?" Chicken Boy cackled. "I gather that your idea of cleaning a desk is to sweep it with your eyes!"

"Ha-ha," I said. "Listen, Gordon. Why don't you make like a magician and disappear?" I tried to go around him, but he blocked my path.

Ms. Foster looked up from her desk. "Is there a problem?" she asked.

"Yes," I said, glad for her help. "Gordon won't let me go out to recess."

"She hasn't finished cleaning her desk," Gordon protested.

"Yes, I have!" I shot back.

"Hmm," said Ms. Foster. "There does seem to be a problem."

Now she would tell Gordon to let me go, I thought. But I should have known better.

"As I understand things, it's now Gordon's responsibility to help you become better organized," Ms. Foster said. Then she and Chicken Boy traded smiles.

Can you believe it? I had to go back to my desk, dump everything out, and go through my stuff one thing at a time. Gordon made me try out all my markers and throw away the dried-out ones, and I had to look through every single paper to find my missing math assignments.

Josh was *definitely* going to wonder why I'd missed recess again. He'd never believe I'd gotten lost or *really* been hiding in the rest room. How was I ever going to explain?

5
"Backpack *What?*"

Luckily we were so busy in class the rest of the day, I didn't *have* to talk to Josh. I think he tried to get my attention a couple of times, but I just acted like I didn't notice, like I was working really hard.

It was the longest Monday ever, but finally it ended. I was worried that Josh would wait for me and try to talk to me after school, but he was out the door as soon as the bell rang.

I was still getting ready to go when Gordon stopped by my desk. "I think I should examine your assignment calendar," he said. That's this sheet Ms. Foster gives us each month that we're supposed to write our homework assignments on.

"I don't use it," I told Gordon. "I just *remember* the homework."

"Oh, really?" Gordon said, tsk-tsking.

I wish he'd stop that. If he were a REAL chicken, I'd *barbecue* him! "Okay, okay," I moaned. "I'll *make* a dumb calendar."

Chicken Boy stood over me as I began to copy down the assignments from the board.

"You don't need to stay and watch," I told him. "I *know* how to write."

He went back to his seat.

When I'd finished copying down the assignments, I stuffed my notebook into my backpack and headed for the door. I hoped I could sneak out before Gordon noticed I was leaving, but no such luck.

"Wait a minute," he said. "I believe a backpack check would be wise."

Reluctantly, I turned around. "A backpack *what*?"

"A backpack check. I want to make certain you have everything you need for your homework tonight. You do want that pizza, don't you?"

"I'd trade a giant-sized double-cheese pizza for mozzarella-covered dog food if you'd just leave me alone," I grumbled as I unzipped my backpack. I checked my calendar, and, wouldn't you know, I had to go back to my desk for my spelling book.

When at last I got outside, there was Josh, standing right outside the door. He'd waited for me after all. "Where were you during afternoon recess?" he asked. "I thought we were finally going to play wall-ball."

"Uh, well, Ms. Foster made me stay in and do some stuff," I mumbled. That much I could tell him without giving away Gordon's and my secret deal.

Josh looked at me suspiciously. "Weren't you talking to Gordon just now?"

I gulped. He'd seen us! "You mean, *Chicken Boy?*" I said. Then I told Josh how I gave Gordon that name because he tsks like a chicken pecking seeds and his eyes get round like chicken eggs when he's afraid of getting into trouble. When he's *being* a chicken, that is.

"I bet he'll lay an egg someday," I said. Josh laughed, and I breathed a sigh of relief.

*   *   *

That night, I'd just finished dinner when Gordon called. "I'm coming over," he said.

"You know where I live?" I said in surprise.

"Certainly," he said. "The phone book is a wonderful tool. I only live a few blocks away. I should be there in five minutes." And he hung up before I could say another word.

I never knew he lived so close. I supposed it was too much to hope he'd get lost on the way.

"Who was that?" Mom asked as she lifted Melanie down from her high chair.

"A boy from my class. Gordon." I said. "He's coming over."

"Are you working on a project together?" she asked.

I nodded, but I didn't tell her the project was *me*.

35

When the doorbell rang, Mom was in the bathroom, giving Melanie a bath. "I'll get it!" I yelled.

"I've already done my homework," I said when I opened the door.

"That's admirable." Gordon stepped into the house. "Let's see it."

"You're not Ms. Foster, you're my *secretary*," I reminded him as he followed me into the living room.

"Tsk, tsk. I'm not going to evaluate it. I just want to check that you've got it."

"Well, of course I've got it." I glared at him as I crossed to the dining room table and picked up my backpack. "It's right here." I unzipped the pack and rummaged inside. "Oh. Uh. Wait a minute." My face began to feel warm. "I think maybe I left it downstairs."

I ran downstairs and got the assignment,

then stuffed it into my backpack. "Okay," I said, "you can leave now."

But Chicken Boy didn't budge. "Have you set out clean clothes? You need to make a timely departure tomorrow."

I rolled my eyes. Why couldn't *he* make a "timely departure" right now! I frowned. "I'll find something to wear in the morning."

Gordon folded his arms. "I think not."

"Know something?" I said. "You remind me of a fly —"

"That's right," Gordon interrupted. "And I intend to *keep* bugging you until you are completely prepared." He took a step down the hall toward the bedrooms. "Perhaps you would like *me* to select tomorrow's garments?"

Garments? "Stay out of my room!" I shouted, jumping in front of him. No way was

he going to see the dirty underwear covering my floor. "Stay here," I said as I stomped down the hall.

I scooped up all the dirty clothes and threw them into my hamper. Then I folded a nearly clean T-shirt and placed it on top of a pair of pants. I opened the door a crack. "See," I said, showing him the "garments."

"Excellent," he said. But he wouldn't leave till I'd found my shoes and put them next to the door and set my alarm clock for fifteen minutes earlier than usual. Argh! All this organization is going to *kill* me.

6
Hide-and-no-seek

I would never admit it to Gordon, but it *was* easier getting ready for school the next morning. I didn't have to search for clothes. My homework was in my backpack. And my shoes were waiting by the front door. I was ready so early I decided to catch a few cartoons before I left. I'd just turned on the TV when the doorbell rang.

"Get your shoes on, and let's go," Gordon said, bossier than ever.

"It's too early to leave," I protested. "Besides, I'm watching a cartoon."

"And if I hadn't arrived to fetch you, you'd have kept watching and been late," Gordon said.

"Would not," I said.

Gordon didn't say another word. He just stood there making chicken-pecking noises till I was ready to go.

"Know something, Gordon?" I said as we walked along the sidewalk. "If you played hide-and-seek, no one would look for you." It was Josh's and my favorite insult.

"I know," Gordon said.

I stopped walking to stare at him. "You do?"

Gordon shrugged. "It's occurred before."

"Really?" I said. "You played hide-and-seek, and no one came to find you?"

Gordon shrugged. "I guess they just didn't want to play with me."

"Well, I think that's pretty mean," I said. Then I blinked. Shoot! I didn't even *like* Gordon, and here I was feeling sorry for him.

We passed by the portable classroom at the edge of the playground, then walked across the playground to our room. Ms. Foster was so pleased to see me on time, she let *me* collect the homework.

As Gordon passed me his spelling, Josh sneaked up beside me. "Ms. Foster's letting *you* collect papers?" he said. "What did you bribe her with?" Then he grinned at Gordon. "How'd you lose your job? Get in trouble or something?"

Gordon ignored him.

Josh turned back to me. "Looks like the teacher's pet lost his voice."

"Aw, leave him alone, Josh," I said.

Josh looked surprised. Then he got mad. "If *you* like Gordon so much, then why don't you *marry* him?"

I glared at Josh. "I don't like him," I said quickly. "But you were being mean."

Josh laughed. "Me, mean? I thought we were friends. How come I saw you walking to school with *him* this morning?"

I sucked in my breath. He'd *seen* us?

Before I could think how to explain, Ms. Foster called, "Hilary! Where are those spelling papers?"

"Coming," I said, and I hurried to collect the rest. I'd just have to work out how to smooth things over with Josh later.

Sure that Gordon would stop by before

recess to check my desk, I stacked my books carefully, threw away a couple of old papers, and put my markers back in my pencil box. No way was I going to miss recess today and give Josh even more to be mad at me about.

I was surprised when Gordon didn't come by.

7
Mozzarella-covered Dog Food

When I walked out onto the playground, Josh was waiting for me. He didn't say a word about Gordon, just stood there bouncing a yellow ball up and down. "Beat you at wall-ball," he said.

"Not a chance." I grabbed the ball away on the next bounce and ran with it across the playground, past the hopscotch courts and the jungle gym.

Josh chased after me. "Hey, come back."

I laughed and ran faster. "You're so slow you couldn't catch a cold!" I shouted. It felt good to be kidding around with him. Like old times.

Josh put on a burst of speed and caught up to me. "Got you!" he yelled, tagging my elbow.

"Took you long enough," I said, stopping.

We walked back to the wall-ball court. I served first, bouncing the ball, then smacking it hard. It struck the ground, then hit the brick wall of the school and bounced deep into the court. Josh had to run backward to get it. His return was weak. This time I hit the ball gently so Josh would have to run up close to the wall to return it.

Then, out of the corner of my eye, I saw Gordon. He stood in back of the group of kids behind Josh and me, watching us play. I smiled at him, but he didn't smile back. Instead, he turned and walked away. Looking after him, I missed my next shot.

"You're out!" Josh yelled. Clasping his hands together, he waved them around in the air. "At last, I am the champion!"

"Not for long," I said. "I'll beat you next time."

Carl stepped up to play Josh, and I ran after Gordon.

"Hey!" I called out as he came even with the jungle gym. "Wait up! I need to talk to you."

Gordon turned around.

"How come you didn't check my desk before recess?" I asked him. "I cleaned it real good."

"If you cleaned it *well*," Gordon said, "then I don't need to check it, right?"

"But that's your job," I said. "I mean, you're my *secretary*."

"Actually," Gordon said, stuffing his hands into his pockets, "I'm considering quitting."

"Quitting?" I said. That would have been good news yesterday. But now I wasn't so sure.

"How come?" I asked. "What about the Pizza Pit?"

Gordon ducked as a stray ball flew over his head. "You don't care about the pizza, remember? As I recall, you said you'd trade a giant-size double-cheese one for mozzarella-covered dog food if I'd just leave you alone."

I kicked a pebble across an empty hop-scotch court. "I was *kidding*," I said. "I didn't really mean it."

"And what you said to Josh?" Gordon asked. "Were you kidding then, too?"

I frowned. "What are you talking about?"

Gordon stared at the ground. "You said you didn't like me."

"Oh."

Gordon sighed. "It's true, isn't it? The other kids don't like me much, either. Because I'm the teacher's pet. Like Josh said."

"Well, there might be other reasons," I said, before I thought how that sounded.

Gordon gave me a hurt look.

Argh! Now I'd gone and made things *worse*. I rushed to explain. "What I mean is, I don't think kids mind that much if you do stuff for Ms. Foster. If they do, they're just jealous."

Gordon frowned. "You said there were *other* reasons."

I stared at a girl hanging upside down on the jungle gym. "Well, sometimes you act like you know everything. And you *can* be a little bossy."

Gordon raised an eyebrow.

"Those things don't bother me as much as they used to," I said quickly. "Because you really are helping me. But other kids might mind more."

Gordon perked up a little. "Then you *do* think I'm helping you?"

I smiled. "I wasn't tardy today, was I? And you really should see my desk."

"Okay," Gordon said. "I'll check it as soon as recess ends."

I grinned. "Does that mean you'll go on being my secretary?"

"I guess so," Gordon said. "Unless you

really do prefer mozzarella-covered dog food to pizza."

I made a face. "Not on your life."

As the bell rang we headed for the classroom. Just as we reached the door, Josh pushed past us. He was muttering something that sounded like "kissy, kissy."

I sighed. I had a feeling that being friends with Josh and Gordon at the same time was not going to be easy.

8
Love Stuff

At lunchtime I was sitting at my desk, eating my bologna sandwich, when Josh passed by. He didn't even look at me. Instead, he whispered something to Alicia, who sits just in front of me. She tossed her head so that the cat earrings she always wears made a jangly sound. Then she looked back at me and giggled.

A cold lump settled into my stomach. I

watched Josh move around the room, stopping at other kids' desks. After a while I heard chanting.

Gordon and Hilary
sitting in a tree
k-i-s-s-i-n-g

Giggles erupted around me. "Hilary loves Gordon," someone hissed. "Pass it on."

I couldn't believe Josh would do this to me! We'd been best friends since this day in first grade when Josh brought a garter snake to school and it got loose. When the snake turned up in some girl's desk, she screamed and would have hit it with her shoe if I hadn't rescued the poor snake. Josh said I was the only girl he knew who wasn't afraid of snakes.

I put my fingers in my ears so I wouldn't

have to listen to what kids were saying, but that didn't get rid of the lump in my stomach.

At lunch recess I stayed away from Josh. If he had been any other boy, I would've just walked up and slugged him. But Josh was my *friend*, and once someone's your friend, you can't treat them like just anybody.

I avoided the other kids, too. Instead of playing wall-ball, I walked around the edge of the playground by myself. Once, to my surprise, I saw Gordon standing by the jungle gym talking to Josh. I wondered what Gordon could be saying. Whatever it was, it must have helped, because I didn't hear anymore "kissy" stuff from Josh or anyone else the rest of the day.

Just before the final bell rang, I cleaned up my desk. I almost forgot to check my calendar for homework assignments, but then I remembered.

I expected Gordon would check my back-pack, so I made sure I had everything for homework that night. But when the bell rang, Gordon scooted past me and out the door so fast I thought a tiger must be chasing him.

As I started walking across the play-ground toward home, I saw Josh over by the portable classroom, practicing wall-ball. I was surprised because I thought it was against the rules to play there. Josh might have been hanging around to talk to me — he knew I usually passed by there — but I didn't feel like talking to him. Not yet, anyhow. So I went home a different way.

The phone rang almost as soon as I ar-rived.

"It's me," said Gordon.

"I know," I said. "How come you left so fast? You didn't check my backpack."

"Well, did you get everything?" he asked.

"I think so," I said.

"Good." There was a pause, then Gordon said, "I didn't want Josh to see me speaking with you."

"Why?"

"You know," Gordon said. "That love stuff."

"Oh." I blushed. Fortunately Gordon couldn't see me, since we were on the phone.

"I asked him to leave you alone," Gordon went on. "I said that you didn't really like me."

"I didn't mean it when I said that," I protested.

"I know," Gordon said. "But Josh won't pick on you if he thinks you don't like me. And then the other kids will stop."

I didn't want to admit it, but I knew Gordon was right. It made me mad, though. Why did Josh have to act like that? If he and the other kids got to know Gordon like I was starting to, they'd like him, too. And that's when I got the best idea ever!

"Listen, Gordon," I said. "Don't you want kids to stop picking on you, too? Wouldn't you like to have more friends?"

"Naturally," he said. "But it's like you said. Even though I don't mean to most of the time, I say things that people don't like. Sometimes I even drive my mother crazy, telling her how she could clean better, or improve her cooking, or her grammar, or . . ."

"But that's it!" I interrupted. "If you can help me be more organized, I can help you stop being so . . . so *know-it-all*. Then the other kids will like you better."

There was silence on the other end of the

line. I tapped on the receiver. "Gordon," I said. "Are you there?"

Finally, he said, "So you really think I can change?"

"If *I* can, *you* can," I said. I hoped I was right.

9
The Plan

It was windy and sprinkling as Gordon and I walked to school Wednesday morning. But I was so excited about my plan, I didn't care. I just pulled my jacket hood over my head and let the wind push me along the sidewalk. "Here's my plan," I said, hoping Gordon would think it was as brilliant as I did. "If I hear you acting know-it-all or bossy, I'll give you a signal."

"A signal? What type of signal?" Gordon pulled his hood up, too.

"I'll wiggle my right ear," I said, reaching up to shake it. It was a great idea for a signal.

"All right," said Gordon.

All right? Only all right?? I wished he could be a little more enthusiastic about my plan. But an "all right" from Gordon was probably the same thing as a "fantastic!" from any other person. And that reminded me of something else that might help him make friends. "I think you should try to give more compliments," I said.

"Compliments?"

"Uh-huh. Like telling people when they do a good job cleaning out their desk, for example," I said slyly.

"I see," he said. "So you think I should

tell everyone they do a nice job cleaning out their desks?"

"Ha-ha," I said. "Only if it's true. Otherwise they'll think you're making fun of them. Anyway, you don't want to say the same thing to each person. It has to be special. And you have to *mean* it."

"Okay, okay," said Gordon. "I'll try." When we were almost to school, he slowed down and stopped. "You want to go on by yourself?" he asked, his face turning red. "I'll understand if you don't want us to walk together."

I hesitated, thinking about Josh. Would he get all mad again if he saw me with Gordon? But Gordon was my friend now, too. "Hey," I said. "Friends stick together."

Gordon smiled. Together we entered the classroom and took our seats. I looked around for Josh, but he wasn't there. When the morning bell rang he still hadn't come. I couldn't help feeling relieved. With Josh absent, it'd be a lot easier to try out my plan.

　＊　　＊　　＊

On Wednesday mornings we go to the library. When we lined up to leave the classroom, I was right behind Gordon, who was

65

right behind Alicia. As we walked down the hall, he accidentally bumped into Alicia. She turned. "Why don't you watch where you're going?"

Gordon sniffed. "Perhaps you should walk a little faster."

"Ahem," I said. Gordon looked over his shoulder at me. I grabbed my ear and wiggled it.

"Oh," Gordon said, slowing down beside me. Alicia walked faster. I could tell she was mad because her back was all stiff.

"Apologize!" I hissed as we hurried to catch up with her. "Then say something nice."

"Like what?" Gordon said.

"Oh, uh, I don't know. What if you — how about if you say you like her earrings?"

"Oh, all right." We reached Alicia, and Gordon tapped her on the shoulder.

Her earrings jingled as she whirled

around. "What do you want?" She glared at him.

"I — I — just wanted to apologize," Gordon stuttered. "I — I didn't mean to step on you." He took a deep breath. "You have nice earrings," he said. "I like cats."

Alicia blinked. "Oh, uh, thanks. My grandma gave them to me."

"Does your grandma like cats?"

"Oh, yes. And so do I. I have this one cat named Snooky who . . ."

I grinned. Gordon and Alicia talked about cats all the rest of the way to the library.

At morning recess I convinced Gordon to play wall-ball. It was still windy outside, but at least it had stopped sprinkling.

"Why'd you go and invite *him*?" Carl complained. He slammed a ball against the brick wall of the school.

"Just give him a chance," I said.

Gordon and I watched the other kids play while we stood in line waiting for our turns. Carl served. An older boy from another class returned the serve with a powerful smash. The ball bounced off the wall and landed just inside the sideline. Carl missed the return and was out.

"He should've anticipated where the ball would land and moved more quickly," Gordon commented as Carl left the court.

Carl heard him and scowled.

I grabbed my ear and wiggled it.

"On the other hand," said Gordon, "what do I know? I probably would've missed that return, too."

Carl relaxed. When it was Gordon's turn to play, he even gave Gordon some pointers. Turns out he didn't need to, though. Gordon was *good* at wall-ball. Before the bell rang, he beat the next three kids in line.

"Hey, where did you learn to play so well?" I asked on our way back to class.

"I've been practicing," he said. "At home."

"Then why haven't you played at recess?"

Gordon shrugged. "No one ever wanted me to."

Carl trotted up behind us. "Nice going," he said to Gordon.

Gordon smiled. "Thanks for the pointers."

"You might even be able to beat Josh," Carl said.

It was the same thought I'd had. And if it was true, Josh wasn't going to like it one bit.

10
Josh Comes Back

As we hung up our jackets at the coatracks the next morning, I reminded Gordon that it was Thursday. "You know what that means, don't you?"

"No, what?" he said.

"It means tomorrow is *Friday*."

"Yes," Gordon agreed. "Friday usually comes after Thursday."

"Argh!" I exclaimed. "Have you forgotten about our deal with Dr. Wentworth?"

Gordon grinned. "Of course not. You *did* remember the social studies report that's due today, right?"

I panicked — until I realized he was teasing. There was no social studies report. I socked him in the shoulder as we walked to our desks. "Don't *do* that to me!"

"Sorry," he said, rubbing his shoulder.

Right off the bat, Ms. Foster asked Gordon to run an errand to the office before the bell rang.

Josh was back. I decided to act like everything between us was normal, hoping that things really would be. I walked up to his desk. "So what did you do yesterday while you were skipping school?" I teased.

Josh sneezed. "Ah-choo!" He wiped his

nose. "Mom made me stay home because I had a temperature."

"You sound like you have a cold."

"Yeah, but my temperature was normal this morning. So Mom said I had to come to school. I'm just not supposed to run around at recess."

"That's too bad," I said. "I guess that means you won't be able to play wall-ball today."

"Lucky you," Josh said. "You won't get beat till tomorrow!"

Carl, who sits across from Josh, leaned toward us. "She might still get beat."

"By you?" Josh grinned. "Not likely."

"No," Carl said. "By Gordon."

"Gordon?" Josh stared at Carl and then turned to me. "Gordon doesn't play wall-ball," he said finally.

I shrugged. Before I could say anything, Carl said, "He does, too. He played yesterday, and he's pretty good."

Josh looked at me suspiciously. "Where did Gordon learn to play wall-ball?"

I shrugged again. "He's been practicing at home."

"He has?" Carl looked disappointed. I guess he'd thought the only reason Gordon had played so well yesterday was because of his coaching.

"So Gordon plays wall-ball," Josh said. I could tell by the look in his eyes that he didn't like the idea at all. Especially if Gordon was any good.

When Gordon came back, Ms. Foster asked him to pass out the math time tests. I couldn't believe it when he said, "Maybe someone else could help today."

Ms. Foster looked a little surprised, but then she picked Alicia, who was waving her hand wildly. As she gave Gordon his test, Alicia smiled. Gordon looked over at me, and I gave him a thumbs-up. I was ready for the test this time, and I'm pretty sure I aced it. Level B, here I come!

At recess, Gordon beat five kids at wall-ball before I finished him off with a great double serve. Josh stood watching from behind the line of kids who were waiting to play. He did not look happy. When the bell rang to go in, he stopped me.

"How come you keep playing with Chicken Boy?" he said. "Aren't *we* friends?"

Even though it was just a few days, it seemed like a long time since I'd thought of Gordon as Chicken Boy. "I don't think we should call him that," I said. "He's not that bad once you get to know him. Can't we *all* be friends?"

Josh glowered at me. "No way."

I glowered back. "Then that's too bad," I said. "Because I'm not going to choose between you."

11
The Challenge

"Meet me outside on the sidewalk to-morrow morning at eight thirty-five," I told Gordon when he called me that night. "And no reminders. I'm going to do this myself."

"Okay," Gordon agreed.

I set my alarm for even earlier than I'd been getting up, stacked some clean clothes on the floor by my bed, and made sure my homework was in my backpack, ready to go.

As I was brushing my teeth, I remembered I didn't know where my shoes were. I found them downstairs in the family room by the couch and set them beside the front door.

Just before I fell asleep, I thought about Josh. Even though I was mad at him and thought he'd been acting really stupid, I missed him. He hadn't wiggled his ears for me since Monday! Maybe he wouldn't mind so much about me being friends with Gordon if he knew why we'd become friends in the first place.

After tomorrow, Gordon's and my deal with Dr. Wentworth would be over. Maybe then, if Gordon agreed, I'd tell Josh about it. Till then, Josh would just have to wait. Nothing was going to stop me from proving I could win that pizza lunch.

When my alarm went off the next morning, I rolled over and shut it off. I'd almost drifted off to sleep again when suddenly I remembered what day it was and forced myself awake.

I dressed quickly, ate a bowl of Corn Crunchies, and was out on the sidewalk in front of my house before Gordon even arrived. Shivering, I zipped up my jacket against the cool morning air.

"What took you so long?" I teased Gordon when he finally appeared. "I've been ready for hours."

Gordon checked his watch. "It's only

eight twenty-five," he said, looking surprised. "I'm ten minutes early."

"Really?" I hadn't thought I was *that* early. But then, I'd never found my lost watch.

"Bet you didn't think I'd make it," I said as we started off.

Gordon smiled. "I was sure you *would*."

That made me feel good. "What's your favorite kind of pizza?" I asked.

"Pepperoni," he said. "I already know yours. Double cheese, right?"

I nodded, blushing. He must've remembered my dog food remark.

As we neared the school, a banging noise came from behind the portable classroom. It sounded like a ball was being thrown against the side of it. Could Josh be practicing again?

"Just a minute," I said to Gordon. I sneaked around to investigate.

It *was* Josh. "What are you doing here?" I asked.

"What does it *look* like I'm doing?" he said, smashing the ball against the wall.

"I thought the portable was off-limits for wall-ball," I said. "Won't you get in trouble if the recess teacher catches you?"

"That's just a *recess* rule," Josh said, hitting the ball again as it bounced toward him. "I play here before and after school lots of times."

Really? Then I remembered he'd played here a few days ago.

Josh caught the ball and held onto it. "I'll play you a game."

"No," I said, shaking my head. "I don't want to be late."

Josh grinned. "I can beat you fast."

Just then Gordon came around the corner.

Josh groaned. "What's Chicken Boy doing here?" he said in a low voice. "Is he with you?"

I rolled my eyes. "Stop calling him Chicken Boy," I whispered.

But Josh wouldn't listen. "Chicken Boy! Chicken Boy!" he shouted.

Gordon glanced around as if to say, "Who? Me?"

"Didn't you know?" Josh said. "That's Hilary's name for you."

"No, it's not," I said, blushing. "I mean, that was before. Before I really knew you."

Gordon looked sad. "Chicken Boy?"

"Because you're afraid of getting in trouble and you're always making chicken pecking noises," Josh said. "You say 'tsk, tsk' all the time."

I cringed. If only Josh would shut up!

Gordon seemed confused. "I do?"

"Sure," Josh said. "Hilary thinks some-day you're going to lay an egg."

"No, I don't!" I protested. Josh was making things worse and worse.

Gordon looked at me as if he knew I was lying.

"I don't think that anymore," I said weakly.

"Hey, Chicken Boy," Josh said, bouncing his ball. "I hear you're pretty good at wall-ball. Want to play?"

"We're not supposed to be here," Gordon said.

"Uh-oh," Josh said, grinning at me. "Chicken Boy is afraid of getting into trouble. Or maybe he's just afraid I'll beat him."

Gordon's jaw tightened. I'd never seen him look so mad. "All right," he said. "Let's play."

12
Chicken Power

"Come on, Gordon," I said, taking a step away from the portable. "We'll be late. You can play Josh later."

Gordon glanced at his watch. "We've got time. But you can go on if you want to."

I sighed. "I'll wait." I stood behind them to watch. A cool breeze blew through my jacket, and I wrapped my arms around myself to keep warm.

Josh threw Gordon the ball. "I'll let you serve first, since I'm going to beat you anyway."

"We'll just see about that." Gordon caught the ball and bounced it up and down a few times. Then he lobbed it hard so that it bounced once on the ground in front of him, then smacked against the side of the portable.

"Good serve!" I yelled.

Josh grunted. With his fingers laced together, he waited till the ball hit the ground and bounced up, then gave it a crashing blow that sent it down to the ground again. It spiraled up to hit the wall.

Nice return, I almost said. But since I was mad at Josh, I didn't.

The ball fell to the ground close to the wall, and Gordon ran up to hit it.

He and Josh smacked the ball back and forth at least twenty times before Gordon hit

85

a return that smashed into the wall without bouncing on the ground first.

"That's it for you!" Josh smirked. "Now it's *my* serve." He smacked the ball hard. The return was long, and Gordon had to scoot way back to get it. He got in a good shot though, and when Josh returned the ball, it went out-of-bounds.

"Tsk, tsk," I said, without really meaning to.

Gordon looked at me in surprise.

I raised my fist in the air. "Chicken power!" I yelled.

Josh frowned. "Oh, great. Chicken Boy AND Chicken Girl."

Just then I heard a faint but shrill ring.

My stomach knotted up. "The bell! Now we really *are* late!"

Gordon glanced at his watch. "It's just the warning bell. We've still got five more minutes."

My stomach relaxed some. Holding up one finger I said, "One minute. Then we've *got* to go in. And you know why."

Josh raised an eyebrow, but I didn't explain.

"Make me a deal, Josh," Gordon said. "If I win on this serve, you won't make fun of me anymore."

Josh snorted. "And if you *don't* win?"

"Just play!" I shouted, and I began to count down from sixty.

"Okay, okay," said Josh.

Gordon eyed the wall carefully, then hit a fast serve that bounced low off the wall.

Counting silently, I watched Josh run toward the ball. He almost didn't get there in time, and his return was weak.

"Forty-eight, forty-seven, forty-six," I whispered.

Gordon was ready. He lobbed the ball hard. When it hit the wall, the ball spun sideways. Before Josh could get to it, the ball hit the ground twice.

"Forty-three!" I yelled. "Game's over!"

"I win!" Gordon shouted.

"*This* time," said Josh.

"Argh!" I said. "You never give up."

Josh actually grinned. He admires anyone who is good at sports, and I knew Gordon's playing had impressed him. "I never knew chickens could play such great wall-ball," he said.

"Tsk, tsk," said Gordon. "Never underestimate the power of a chicken."

Maybe there was hope for the three of us yet.

Together we rounded the corner of the portable and started to walk across the playground. Suddenly, I froze. "If that was the first bell," I said, "how come we're the only ones outside?"

13
A Deal's a Deal

Gordon looked at his watch. "That's funny," he said. "According to my watch we've still got five more minutes."

"But that's what you said just before you and Josh finished your game," I reminded him.

Gordon stared at his watch. His eyes grew round. "The second hand's not moving. It's — it's *dead*."

"Run for it!" I yelled. But even as our feet pounded across the playground, I knew it was too late. The final bell had already rung. I felt like throwing up. I knew that both Dr. Wentworth and Ms. Foster would be disappointed in me, and I was disappointed, too.

"It's my fault we're late," Gordon said as we reached the school doors. "I'm a lousy secretary. Now we won't get to go to the Pizza Pit."

"A lousy *what*?" asked Josh. "The Pizza Pit? What are you talking about?"

So of course we had to explain. We even told him about how I've been helping Gordon stop being so bossy. Josh looked really surprised. He didn't have a clue!

At the office, Mrs. Crawford gave Josh a tardy slip and waved him on to class. But she must have known about Dr. Wentworth's deal with Gordon and me because she said, "You two stay right here. Dr. Wentworth will want to talk with you."

As soon as we saw her, Gordon explained about the wall-ball game and about his watch.

"And I don't have a watch," I said. "I lost it a long time ago."

"I'm very sorry," Dr. Wentworth said. "But a deal's a deal. And you were also breaking a rule, playing by the portable."

I started to tell her that Josh had said it was okay to play there but changed my mind. We were in trouble for being tardy anyway, so what difference did it make?

"You may go back to class now," Dr. Wentworth said. "And would you please ask Ms. Foster to send Josh to speak with me right away?"

Later, after Josh had left for the office,

Dr. Wentworth came down to our room by herself. She and Ms. Foster talked in whispers. Part of me wanted to hear what they were saying, and part of me was glad that I *couldn't* hear.

When the morning recess bell rang, Josh still wasn't back. Ms. Foster looked up from her desk. "Hilary and Gordon, would you come here a moment, please? I'd like to speak with you."

As everyone else raced out of the room for recess, Gordon and I approached Ms. Foster's desk. I was so worried about what she might say, my knees were shaking. I wondered if Gordon felt as nervous as I did.

"I had a talk with Dr. Wentworth," Ms. Foster said, running a hand through her wild hair. "She told me all about what happened. I guess you know now that the portable is off-limits for wall-ball."

We nodded.

Ms. Foster continued. "After talking to Josh, Dr. Wentworth says she's decided to give you a second chance at that pizza."

I couldn't believe it. "Really?"

Ms. Foster smiled a little. "Yes." She looked at Gordon. "She understands about your watch stopping. And she says Josh insisted that the wall-ball game was his idea, and you only played there because he *told* you it was okay."

"But he really *did* think it was okay," I said.

Ms. Foster shook her head. "I don't think so. He's been in trouble for playing by the portable before. Anyway, how about it? Do you think you can be on time all next week?"

"Certainly," Gordon said.

I beamed. "You bet!"

Josh came back to the room at lunchtime. He wouldn't look at me as he walked past me to his seat, so I followed him to the back of the room when he went to get his lunch sack out of his backpack.

"How come you said it was okay to play by the portable when you knew it wasn't?" I asked.

Josh hung his head. "I'm sorry. I *told* Dr. Wentworth it wasn't your fault. I didn't know Gordon was just helping you be on time for school and making sure you got your work turned in. I thought you were doing stuff with him because you were friends."

"But we *are* friends," I said, confused. "I mean, we weren't at first, but we are now."

Josh nodded. "But I didn't know that other stuff till today, and so I was kind of mad because, well, because I thought if you'd decided to be friends with Gordon, it meant you didn't really want to be friends with me anymore."

"Josh," I said. "You've been my best friend since first grade. Gordon's only been my friend for a few *days*. I like him, but he'll never be *you*."

Josh's stick-out ears turned red. "Really?"

"Really," I said. Then I had a great idea. "Know something? You could help me and Gordon if you wanted to."

"How?"

"Well, you could help me remember to turn in my homework assignments."

"I suppose."

He sure didn't sound very excited about the idea. "And if Gordon starts acting bossy or know-it-all," I said, "you could give him the secret signal."

Josh's eyes lit up. "What signal?"

I reached up with my fingers and wiggled my ear. "But you're lucky," I said. "*You* won't even have to use your fingers."

Josh grinned. "It's not as good as winning at wall-ball, but at least I'm better at *something*."

"About the wall-ball," I teased. "Maybe Gordon and I should give you some lessons after school."

"Hey," said Josh. "I'm not as bad as all that!"

"Wanna bet?"

"Let's ask Gordon," said Josh. So we brought our lunches over to Gordon's desk and pulled up two extra chairs like it was something we'd been doing all along.

"Hilary thinks I need wall-ball lessons,"

Josh said as he unwrapped his sandwich. "What do you think?"

Gordon grinned. "As a chicken," he said, "I've usually found that eggs-tra eggs-perience is always a plus."

**Three kids, one wacky friendship . . .
What will they think of next?**

**Find out in *Third-Grade Friends #2
Josh Taylor, Mr. Average***

Hilary and Gordon arrived together at seven. Hilary had brought markers, and Mom found some white construction paper in a cupboard in the family room. We tried to think of things to write on the posters.

Hilary waved a blue marker in the air. "An idea just went through my head."

"That's because there's nothing to stop it," I said.

"Ha-ha," said Hilary. "How's this: 'Vote for Josh, by gosh.'"

"Sounds good," I said.

"How about this one?" said Gordon. "'Don't be a squash, vote for Josh.'"

Hilary and I rolled our eyes.

Gordon shrugged. "There's not a lot of words that rhyme with Josh."

We ended up making three posters using Hilary's idea and two more that just said "*Vote for Josh for Class Representative*." After we finished that last poster I figured we were ready for tomorrow, but Gordon said, "We need something besides posters."

"Like what?" I said.

"I bet Nicola will hand out buttons," said Hilary. "I heard her tell Stephanie her mom had a button machine."

Gordon nodded. "Eggs-actly. That's why we need some kind of gimmick."

"A what-tick?" I asked.

"A gimmick," Gordon repeated. "Something that will really get kids to notice you."

Hilary snapped her fingers. "Josh could wear a costume! . . ."

About the Author

Suzanne doesn't remember ever being tardy to school when she was a kid, and in fact her mother says she was "a perfect child." Suzanne doesn't entirely trust her mother's memory however, as over the years moms tend to forget all the bad stuff — which is probably a good thing.

A former elementary school librarian, Suzanne claims that her ability to stay organized on the job was largely due to her wonderful assistants.

The author of several children's books including the Children's Choice Award–winning picture book, *Library Lil*, Suzanne lives in Renton, Washington, with her husband, Mark, her daughter, Emily, and her son, Ward. You can visit Suzanne on the web at www.suzanne-williams.com.